T0025254

Finding True Love Online:

Ditching the Stigma

Second Edition

Finding True Love Online:

Ditching the Stigma

E. SANYO BOND

TATE PUBLISHING
AND ENTERPRISES, LLC

Finding True Love Online
Copyright © 2014 by E. Sanyo Bond. All rights reserved.

No part of this publication may be reproduced, stored in a retrieval system or transmitted in any way by any means, electronic, mechanical, photocopy, recording or otherwise without the prior permission of the author except as provided by USA copyright law.

The opinions expressed by the author are not necessarily those of Tate Publishing, LLC.

Published by Tate Publishing & Enterprises, LLC
127 E. Trade Center Terrace | Mustang, Oklahoma 73064 USA
1.888.361.9473 | www.tatepublishing.com

Tate Publishing is committed to excellence in the publishing industry. The company reflects the philosophy established by the founders, based on Psalm 68:11,
"The Lord gave the word and great was the company of those who published it."

Book design copyright © 2014 by Tate Publishing, LLC. All rights reserved.

Published in the United States of America

ISBN: 978-1-62746-450-5
1. Family & Relationships / Love & Romance
2. Family & Relationships / Marriage & Long Term Relationships
14.09.12

Dedication

For Matt,

My gift from the Lord and my soul mate.

Sanyo

> *[I am so glad that you are a part of my life. It is such a privilege – to know you, to share myself with you, and to walk together on the paths that takes us in so many beautiful directions. I had heard of "soul mates" before, but I never knew such a person could exist—Until I met you.....]* (Pagels, D. 1950).

Contents

Is looking for love online practical?

Most people are still looking for a fairytale but in today's environment, it can be difficult or very near impossible to find. So, assuming that it is even possible, how do you get it? The 'fairytale' idea in love implies that a person would randomly encounter their soul mate, fall madly in love at first sight, then get married and live happily ever after. Although this scenario can and probably does happen, in today's society it may not be a common occurrence. This is due to the busy lives led by many individuals and the numerous varied paths people take in life. Your ideal mate may not be in a venue that you frequent or vice versa, therefore, your paths may never cross (at least not without a little assistance).

You may have heard of the definition for madness, you know that old saying…the one about doing the same things repeatedly but expecting different results. Well, our environment has changed and continues to change, therefore, our strategy for finding and keeping love needs to adapt for our fairytale to become a reality. We can no longer depend solely on traditional means for finding love if we are serious about long-term companionship. Some of us are still fortunate enough to grow up next door to our soul-mates or even meet him or her in high school, or if not there, even in college. However, those of us who have chosen to pursue careers, jobs, and other priorities ahead of love are finding out that what we want is not next door anymore. We are also realizing that even if the person we want is within our zip code or state, we cannot find the time with our busy schedules to meet, and connect with these people.

Some people still look at finding a mate online as taboo or even as a sign of desperation. If an individual should really give serious consideration to the concept, one would realise that the risks are no different from meeting a stranger next door, or at the grocery store, bar, or any place other place where you may meet a stranger. Au contraire, looking for love online just makes plain sense. This is especially true if a person is busy and would still like to have a choice of mate. When meeting new people, a person should employ basic common sense; the same is true when seeking love regardless of the venue or the mode of introduction.

In this internet age, our world has become smaller, and our horizons are somewhat expanded when compared to the way the world was in past decades. People have gotten busier and are generally more caught up in the pursuit of financial security, therefore, leaving even less time to actively pursue emotional connections or relationships outside of work. As a result we use technology to communicate with people on a level almost daily, thereby shrinking our world. This reality is compounded by the use of technology such as texting, which further limits the human connection. One thing is certain though, people are still the same, and everybody needs somebody at some point in their lives. Because of the need for human connection, and the recent evolution of the way, people spend their time; more and more individuals are turning to the internet as their means of conducting social interactions and meeting potential long-term mates.

Many who have used the internet to make emotional

connections are familiar with the constant barrage of non-genuine individuals claiming to be looking for love online. Some of these individuals are seeking anything from a financial supporter to a fling or just someone to connect with to act out their perversions. This being said; there are people just like you online looking for someone just like you or similar to you. Because the person is using the internet to make the connection does not in itself mean the individual should be suspected of ill-will or be considered desperate. However, it is helpful if one can find and recognize the right person and then do what it takes to get your man or woman. Although there are many people in the world who cannot be trusted, there are also good people, with good intentions just waiting to make that important connection with someone just like you. This book will help you to recognize the good people when you meet them, teach you how to treat these people and give details about how to build and maintain a great online relationship. So is it practical to look for love online? Absolutely! I would even say it is SMART. The internet is a good resource for making connections, why not use it to find your soul-mate?

I don't have a lot of time to waste on the internet.

Love is something that people look for throughout their lives. Some find it, however; many participate in a lifelong quest with little success. There is a variety of reasons for the lack of success when looking for love, but in order to become one of the people who make meaningful connections with desirable outcomes, one has to know what to look for and what to expect. A person's expectations, about online dating, has as important an impact on the development and success of the relationship, as how much effort one puts into the relationship.

Before getting into the reasons why some peoples struggle to make relationships work, let us look at my story. I married late (by ancient standard) like so many professionals out there, because I did not have the time or desire to focus on a relationship, and because I did not want to become a statistic. After pursuing a career for many years and being successful, I started wanting more, I started to feel incomplete. I not only wanted to be loved and be in love, but I also wanted my own family. I suppose; one can say that my biological clock started to tick rather loudly. It was when I came to that realization that I decided to focus my attention on my personal life. After all, we succeed at the things we work at the most. Success is not so sweet when it is a lonely success. I have found that although money makes life more comfortable, it does not act as a good substitute for loved ones and family. To cut to the chase I finally met someone online and got married in a matter of months. Now I am in a relationship with the love of my life; I have an awesome little boy, and not a single regret.

My sister also went through the same process where she met someone online, and she married him within one year. She has also started her own family, and she seems very happy to the point where they are now planning to expand their new family. As wonderful as everything sounds, it was not easy getting to that point. I tried several online dating sites before meeting my husband, but by the time I met him, I had learned a few things about online dating and online dating sites. I found that whether or not the site is free, it does not indicate the quality of people on the site. I have heard people use the logic that they would only use a paid site because if someone could not afford to pay an online dating site membership fee, they probably could not afford to have a spouse. Maybe or maybe not, but frugal is not always a bad thing (just a thought).

I was about ready to give up when I met my husband, but what made our relationship work was not chance, it was the realization that came to me during the process. Interestingly enough, when I met my husband, I had made a conscious decision to work fewer hours than I had in the past, so I had more time on my hands. Having time or making time to pursue an emotional connection is an essential component in beginning the process of meeting and marrying someone whether or not you meet him or her online. Because a person is out of driving distance that does not mean he or she deserves less of your time. If a relationship is to develop and progress, two people must make time to spend with each other. Time spent could be on the phone, on Skype, or in person when possible. If one cannot make the time to properly pursue a relationship, stop wasting the other person's time until you are able to commit to finding love.

How well do I know myself? Do I know who I'm looking for?

Work will take as much time as you give it, it will never end, so whenever a decision is made to start dating or to find that person with whom you wish to spend the rest of your life, it is necessary to commit to focusing on the task. One thing I learned over the years is that the old adage "practice makes perfect" is true. The more time you spend doing something, the better you get at it. This is true in your professional life, and it is as true in your personal life. No matter how terrible you are at meeting people or interacting with people, the more often you do it, the better you get at it. The key is to not become discouraged while you are undergoing the learning process because sometimes it can be challenging. One of the good things about meeting people on the internet is that if you are rejected, you do not have to take it personally because the person/s do not know you. That being said; there are many who are very sensitive to the opinions of others. If you are such a person, one should take extra care when meeting people online. Many of the people one would meet online are superficial and do not care about the feelings of others. Nevertheless, that is true of people in general. Some are more likely to show their unkindness because they lack the face-to-face connection. They do not usually see beyond the faces attached to the profiles. A person cannot be responsible for other people's shortcomings and shortsightedness; therefore, one should disregard those that are substandard in their behavior and move on to individuals with qualities that are more appealing. For this reason, it is very important to recognize the good ones when they come along.

It is difficult, maybe even impossible, for someone to find that right person if one does not have a clear picture of what one wants in a person and from a relationship. It is very rare for someone to just stumble upon the perfect person or relationship. It is easy to overlook or disregard the perfect relationship if one is unaware or unclear about what one is looking for. This may be due to chaotic thoughts or ideas. In other words, finding that special someone has to be approached like a problem that needs to be solved.

Problems are sometimes difficult to solve for a variety of reasons, however, one of the biggest reasons is that people fail to accurately diagnose the problem. The first step in solving a problem is to correctly describe the problem. If one does not know what the real problem is, it makes it a bit more difficult to solve.

To find that special person, one should know exactly what qualities make that person special for you. Generally it is best to seek out actual personal qualities, instead of physical qualities. Physical qualities are easy to find or even achieve, but personal qualities that are compatible to what one may want or need are harder to come by. As a rule, one should be honest with oneself. An individual cannot know what he or she wants nor have a successful long-term relationship with anyone if he or she is not honest with him or herself about what he or she wants from the relationship. Self-evaluation does not require a person to have a negative view of himself; however, it does require a person to look at both negative and positive qualities that one may possess. This honest view would help an individual to more clearly visualize the ideal mate. Not everyone can be truthful when doing self-analysis. Many people tell themselves lies because it makes them feel better about themselves, but that is not going to help you have a successful relationship because eventually the person you are with will find out exactly whom you are. Do not pretend you want a smart or intelligent woman if all you want is a "hot" woman. Do not pretend you want a man with morals if you do not have any or do not believe in morals, it will not work out in the end. If you feel that you may not be good enough for some of the people that you would really like, then, perhaps you are right. That being said; you should choose someone whom you believe is adequate for you because feeling substandard in a relationship is a sure relationship killer. Do not just choose a mate based on the opinion of others. It is better to change yourself and make a choice you are proud of instead of choosing what you think should be "right". What is right in someone else's eyes may be completely wrong for you.

So what do you do when you find that person you are interested in? Be honest, be honest with yourself and be honest with that person. Let them know your hopes, dreams, ideals, and what you want for the future. Be sure to listen to that person as well and evaluate how well your ideals mesh. If you can see that you are opposites in every way, just leave it alone, and move on…it will not work out. It is true that 'opposites attract', but it is also true that 'birds of a feather flock together'. If there are any red flags that are raised when you are getting to know your person, please deal with them. Do not ignore anything. If the information you are getting does not add up, chances are it is false information. Do not make assumptions; be forthright when asking for information. Ask about anything and everything that is important to you. If an individual's ability to provide for a family is your number one priority, ask about that. Do not be afraid to be labeled a 'gold-digger'. Be candid about your concerns and be reasonable about the responses you receive. Remember to ask the same questions in multiple ways because in an effort to impress you, a potential mate may just tell you what they think you want to hear, or what makes them look the best in your eyes. If the answers you are given are not direct or satisfactory, it is best to move on and not waste your time any further on that individual. Be reasonable, do not ask someone for information that he/she cannot give to you (such as a social security number).

Do not become intimate with a potential mate until you are sure that you want to spend your life with that person and until you are sure that that person shares your same feelings. Sex confuses things. It is not to be taken lightly (no matter how grown up one may feel he is). Although it is very possible for one to be very physically attracted to a new person, beware of the person who seems to want to rush the physical element of a relationship without developing the emotional and spiritual bonds that are also required to build the relationship. Having an adult relationship does not mean having a sexual relationship. One of my male friends told me many years ago that if a man truly intends to marry a woman, he would try to get to know her without pushing for sex, because they will have the rest of their lives to engage in the activity. It is not difficult to be caught up in the excitement of meeting a new, attractive person. When this happens, one has to be careful not to confuse attraction with being in love. Love has many feelings attached to it, but love is still very much a decision. While looking for love, an individual would encounter various challenges, especially in this internet age.

Is this really love or is this a scam?

Be prepared to date a few frauds. People with bad intentions are everywhere. They are on the internet, and they are in your local grocery store, next-door, at church; wherever you go. Because one is being honest with oneself that does not mean everyone else is. Since every person will not read this book, it is fair to assume that you will meet some who have some of the same problems you are cautioned about in this book. Being aware of what to look for is what will determine whether one will be seduced by a fraud. Even the most knowledgeable person can be taken in by a con artist if that conman or woman is suave enough. Remember not every person has the same agenda. Although you may be looking for a permanent, long-term relationship with someone special, you may encounter individuals who are looking for the opposite. Some people are honest enough to state that they want only a fling, but in my experience there are still many people who prefer to pretend that they are looking for the love of their lives. They get a thrill from the deception. Some feel that they would encounter less resistance if they used the guise of being interested in a long-term relationship instead of just admitting that they are addicted to the chase and capture of a fling. In some cases, there are people who are looking for the love of their lives, but their method for doing so includes dating and being intimate with multiple persons during the same period. Others are so broken that even if they want to find love, they cannot be open and honest with another individual. Although each person has his or her prerogative to live life as he or she chooses most individuals who are seeking a true and meaningful connection do not appreciate being involved in relationships where one partner dates multiple people. Generally, intimacy clouds one's vision and prevents one from making good decisions. Therefore, it is best to approach intimacy carefully until one is sure of the relationship.

Relationships that begin online can be scary and exciting at the same time. In this internet age, one cannot be too sure that every person he or she meets online is exactly whom they purport to be. The internet allows for anonymity, so there is the added risk of meeting persons who have nefarious backgrounds. Despite these facts, the internet and online dating sites provide a vast amount of potential partners to choose from. Sifting through the quagmire of profiles can be a major task for some people and so many resort to just looking at the pictures. This method of selecting a potential partner can be dangerous. Not every picture that is posted belongs to the person posting the photo. Many of the persons who engage in dating fraud actually use photographs of models and other beautiful people from magazines worldwide because they realize that beautiful faces and bodies attract the most attention. It is important to remember that most of the people on these profiles use the best photographs at their disposal. Some of these photos may be current, and some may be seriously outdated. In fact the better looking the picture, the more skeptical one ought to be, because con artists tend to use glamour shots and shots of models to carry out their schemes. This is not to say one should choose an ugly or less desirable looking person, it simply means that one should not use physical appearance as the sole reason for wanting to get to know a person better. Keep in mind that beauty is in the eye of the beholder, so do not expect everyone to see eye to eye with one's idea of who is beautiful. Try looking at the profiles for ones that are more detailed and complete. If the profile seems interesting, try to get to know the person and perhaps confirm the things that are written in the profile. Remember people will write in their profiles what they want you to know, and what would make them look the best. Those two things do not always add up to the truth.

One should always exercise caution when

contacting, meeting, and giving personal information to someone he or she does not know. Employ the same tactics you would use if you met a complete stranger at your local market. Seeing a person's face does not make them trustworthy or safe, so when meeting someone online ignore the face and treat the person like any other stranger. Remember a person's look can be very deceptive. Many criminals or dishonest people do not look like criminals or dishonest; they look like ordinary people you meet everyday. If one is looking for a certain type of mate, one should be sure to find the profiles indicating the type of mate then choose the faces one would want to match the potential mate. Never choose the face and hope to work on the profile; do it the other way around. It must be noted though that no matter how beautiful a person may be on the inside, and sometimes it is difficult to get past the exterior.

There is a particular scenario that has played out repeatedly in my online dating experience. I would be contacted by a very handsome man. He would tell me how wonderful he thinks I am and very quickly (usually within the first or second contact) he would express interest in becoming my husband. These men all had one thing in common, they all listed their home addresses as being somewhere in the USA, yet they all seem to be overseas somewhere because of a family tragedy; or a job. Usually, they are somewhere in Nigeria because of the death of a family member or they got transferred there because of their job, but they may also be in Germany, Spain, or England. It doesn't usually take long before these people tell you about their family tragedy, then they prey on your sympathetic nature and ask for monetary help. This is a scam. Women do it, and men do it. Many men and women have lost thousands of dollars to these scammers on online dating sites. People are looking for love and generally want to be open-minded; this makes them more vulnerable and therefore susceptible to these scammers. According to Bob Sullivan at MSNBC, "So-called Nigerian scams, where victims are ultimately tricked into sending money to the African country using some irreversible method like a wire transfer, are common. The Secret Service and other U.S. agencies have issued warnings on the scams, also known as "419" or "advance-fee" frauds. But the seductive flavor of this type of the scam — known to some as "sweetheart scams" — and the incredible patience shown by the scammer reveal just how far con artists will go to trick their marks." Sweetheart scams, although popular via international agents, are also very possible and common nationally. The scammers employ similar tactics as the Nigerian scammers; however, they may come to visit prior to asking for money. They may even ask you for money so that they can come to visit. Do yourself a favor and decide at that juncture if that is the type of relationship you desire.

Whenever possible, select profiles of individuals who live within a reasonable driving distance of your location, however, if you have no real reason to remain in your current location, you should consider extending your search for a potential partner countrywide. This is a case where being honest with oneself is important. If you love where you live and never want to move, be sure to disclose that information to any potential mates because for some this is a deal breaker. Although it is possible to take it a step further and seek an international mate, one must be extremely careful because profiles from certain countries (namely the USA) are targeted, for fraudulent activity, more than others. If you know, you will have a problem facilitating a relationship that is a farther distance away than your state, do not indicate interest, or accept contacts from people who are outside of your distance range. Many people believe that long-distance relationships do not work out but according to www. longdistancerelationships.com, the research shows statistically speaking, that they are no less successful than relationships that are not long-distance. The idea here is not to use distance as an excuse or a barrier when choosing a potential mate.

One of my girlfriends met a handsome man (by general standards) online (there are many of them) and they hit it off right away. His being easy to look at fueled her interest. He said all of the right things and he did almost all of the right things however, his story just did not make sense. It was obvious that he was giving the version of things that would elicit the most sympathy and that he was telling her the things that made him look the best in her eyes. Therefore, she fell for it; at least for a while. My friend empathized with this man, and she had started to develop strong feelings for him. She was also taken in because his story was one of misfortune. He lived in one of the most impoverished cities in the country, and he was struggling to educate himself while working. She understood that kind of struggle because she had done it herself and knew it could be trying without the right support. According to him, he had to leave home when he was in his early teens because of abuse from his stepfather. That was his story. His story did not include what he had been doing since then, but he also revealed that he lived with his grandmother or an uncle sometimes. This man turned out to be a shyster. Yes, he had a difficult life, but not for any of the reasons he stated.

During the process of getting to know this fellow, my friend decided to try to help him find a job (since he could not do it on his own). She paid to have his resume professionally done, and all he had to do was send it in to perspective employers. This turned out to be too much of a task for the young man to handle, or maybe it was not where his interests lay. Nevertheless, my friend dropped him like a hot potato once she found out that he refused to apply for any jobs. He was quite content telling his story, having people feel sorry for him while his targets were taking care of his financial needs in the process. As it turned out, he really had no real interest in finding employment to take care of himself. His primary job was keeping his physical appearance pristine, so that he could continue to attract people who wanted to take care of him. Although this man did not use an elaborate scam such as the ones common among the Nigerians, his plan was almost as sinister. Please do not waste your time on potential partners like that. The sad part about all this is that there are actually decent people out there who have fallen on misfortune and are just waiting for an opportunity to get back on their feet, but one will find it hard to distinguish between the genuine ones and the ones that just want to take advantage of innocent people who are looking for love.

I have been fortunate (or unfortunate) enough to see multiple persons on Judge Judy and other televisions court shows where they took their previous partners to court over personal loans, property, failure to disclose important information about themselves etc.. At the end of the cases, one of the partners always cautions against getting romantically involved with people one may have met online. This is a sad situation because the mode of meeting the individual gets the blame for the failure of the relationship when in reality the same things may have happened anyway regardless of how they met. They do not take into account the fact that many others go to court for the same reason, with the same outcome, but these others did not meet their ex-partners online. One needs to take heed and be very cautious when it comes to monetary dealings when one is dating anyone. It does not matter if the person was found online or at your dentist's office; money tends to drive a wedge between people especially if one of them is less than honest. According to L. Langemeier, "Lending money to friends or relatives can put a strain on your relationships and even ruin them if, for some reason, the loan is not repaid." If a potential partner asks for money, be sure you are willing to establish the boundaries regarding the transaction and make the terms of the loan clear, otherwise be prepared to give the money away and never see it again. It may also be pertinent to inform the individual that the transaction is a singular deal. Of course, if the person becomes a spouse, whatever happens during a marriage plays out under a different set of rules.

Communication and Culture: Does love really conquer all?

If one should choose to date internationally or outside of one's immediate culture (as is becoming more prevalent), it is important to note that special considerations should be made during communication. Lantieri and Patti wrote, ["Culture" is often at the root of communication challenges. Our culture influences how we approach problems, and how we participate in groups and in communities. When we participate in groups we are often surprised at how differently people approach their work together.

Culture is a complex concept, with many different definitions. But, simply put, "culture" refers to a group or community with which we share common experiences that shape the way we understand the world. It includes groups that we are born into, such as gender, race, or national origin. It also includes groups we join or become part of. For example, we can acquire a new culture by moving to a new region, by a change in our economic status, or by becoming disabled. When we think of culture this broadly, we realize we all belong to many cultures at once.] Many find persons from different cultures appealing because they like the 'exotic' flavor. This is fine, however, when things start to become serious in a relationship, and one has to go beyond the surface; one may find out that the differences are insurmountable. Sometimes, the differences are just too great. These differences may be as simple as food choices, or as complex as marital customs and choices.

It is easier to have misunderstandings across cultures than within cultures. Even if there is a common language, the words and do not always carry the same meanings across cultures. Because of this, relationships that encompass different cultures require patience and a willingness to understand each other, otherwise there can be an abundance of hurt feelings and a ruined relationship. In today's culture of instant gratification, it is rare to find persons who have the ability to exhibit the necessary patience that is required with intercultural relationships. Any relationship demands patience to some degree and lack of patience is a sure relationship damper. According to Dupraw and

Axner, [there are six fundamental patterns of cultural differences -- ways in which cultures, tend to vary from one another -- are described below. As you enter into multicultural communications, keep these generalized differences in mind. If you find yourself in a confusing situation, and you suspect that cross-cultural differences are at play, try asking yourself how culture may be shaping your own reactions, and try to see the world from others' points of view.

1.Different Communication Styles The way people communicate varies widely between, and even within, cultures. One aspect of communication style is language usage. Across cultures, some words and phrases are used in different ways. For example, even in countries that share the English language, the meaning of "yes" varies from "maybe, I'll consider it" to "definitely so," with many shades in between.

Another major aspect of communication style is the degree of importance given to non-verbal communication. Non-verbal communication includes not only facial expressions and gestures; it also involves seating arrangements, personal distance, and sense of time. In addition, different norms regarding the appropriate degree of assertiveness in communicating can add to cultural misunderstandings. For instance, some white Americans typically consider raised voices to be a sign that a fight has begun, while some black, Jewish and Italian Americans often feel that an increase in volume is a sign of an exciting conversation among friends. Thus, some white Americans may react with greater alarm to a loud discussion than would members of some American ethnic or non-white racial groups.

2. Different Attitudes toward Conflict

Some cultures view conflict as a positive thing, while others view it as something to be avoided. In the U.S., conflict is not usually desirable; but people often are encouraged to deal directly with conflicts that do arise. In fact, face-to-face meetings customarily are recommended as the way to work through whatever problems exist. In contrast, in many Eastern countries, open conflict is experienced as embarrassing or demeaning; as a rule, differences are best worked out quietly. A written exchange might be the favored means to address the conflict.

3. Different Approaches to Completing Tasks

From culture to culture, there are different ways that people move toward completing tasks. Some reasons include different access to resources; different judgments of the rewards associated with task completion, different notions of time, and varied ideas about how relationship-building and task-oriented work should go together.

When it comes to working together effectively on a task, cultures differ with respect to the importance placed on establishing relationships early on in the collaboration. A case in point, Asian and Hispanic cultures tend to attach more value to developing relationships at the beginning of a shared project and more emphasis on task completion toward the end as compared with European-Americans. European-Americans tend to focus immediately on the task at hand, and let relationships develop as they work on the task. This does not mean that people from any one of these cultural backgrounds are more or less committed to accomplishing the task or value relationships more or less; it means they may pursue them differently.

4. Different Decision-Making Styles

The roles individuals play in decision-making vary widely from culture to culture. For example, in the U.S., decisions are frequently delegated -- that is, an official assigns responsibility for a particular matter to a subordinate. In many Southern European and Latin American countries, there is a strong value placed on holding decision-making responsibilities oneself. When decisions are made by groups of people, majority rule is a common approach in the U.S.; in Japan consensus is the preferred mode. Be aware that individuals' expectations about their own roles in shaping a decision may be influenced by their cultural frame of reference.

5. Different Attitudes toward Disclosure

In some cultures, it is not appropriate to be frank about emotions, about the reasons behind a conflict or a misunderstanding, or about personal information. Keep this in mind when you are in a dialogue or when you are working with others. When you are dealing with a conflict, be mindful that people may differ in what they feel comfortable revealing. Questions that may seem natural to you -- What was the conflict about? What was your role in the conflict? What was the sequence of events? -- may seem intrusive to others. The variation among cultures in attitudes toward disclosure is also something to consider before you conclude that you have an accurate reading of the views, experiences, and goals of the people with whom you are working.

6. Different Approaches to Knowing

Notable differences occur among cultural groups when it comes to epistemologies -- that is, the ways people come to know things.

European cultures tend to consider information acquired through cognitive means, such as counting and measuring, more valid than other ways of coming to know things. Compare that to African cultures' preference for affective ways of knowing, including symbolic imagery and rhythm. Asian cultures' epistemologies tend to emphasize the validity of knowledge gained through striving toward transcendence.[3]

Recent popular works demonstrate that our own society is paying more attention to previously overlooked ways of knowing.4 Indeed, these different approaches to knowing could affect ways of analyzing a community problem or finding ways to resolve it. Some members of your group may want to do library research to understand a shared problem better and identify possible solutions. Others may prefer to visit places and people who have experienced challenges like the ones you are facing, and get a feeling for what has worked elsewhere.]

You may have heard the saying that 'actions speak louder than words'. This is true. One should always be observant, and never ignore ones instincts. If what someone is, doing does not match what they are saying, then ignore the words, and listen to the actions. It is difficult for body language to lie. Besides, anyone can say anything, but the proof is in the pudding so to speak.

Body language does not lie, however; there are non-verbal cues that do not mean the same things across cultures. Some cultures use their hands more when speaking, while others look at hand gestures as a distraction method. Be careful not to get too caught up in non-verbal cues. Sometimes as yawn is just a yawn.

It is equally important that when you get together that you do not make fun of each other's nuances until there is a deeper understanding of each other's culture. In a perfect world love would be all that matters and everything else would fall into place. In reality, love helps one to be patient enough to learn to communicate especially inter-culturally, however, sometimes love is not yet strong enough and needs the help of clearer communications for the relationship to work. In other words, do not depend on your love to get you through challenges, learning how to understand and communicate with each other makes a world of difference and could even strengthen your love for each other.

What if there is no photo?

If one should receive any form of contact from any individual (unless of course, it is downright offensive), even if the contact does not overtly express interest in getting to know one better, one should not hesitate to begin the process of getting to know that person. The way to look at this is that the person saw something in your profile that attracted them and prompted them to make that first contact. This may seem like a strange piece of advice, but I met my husband that way. He paid me a backhanded compliment while expressing that the physical distance between us was not suitable for what he was looking for. My first thought was 'okay', so he thinks I'm cute, but he is also saying that being such a long distance away makes it impossible for us to even pursue any type of relationship. My second thought was, 'why not find out where he is?' maybe I can at least get a pen-pal out of the contact or at least share some interesting stories. Based on my previous encounters with scammers, I was even thinking that it was another scammer trying to get through. I was prepared to block this person if he even gave the slightest hint that he may be situated in Africa or Europe somewhere. Anyway, these thoughts did not prevent me from pursuing further conversation with him. I felt that I was not losing anything by making contact and finding out a few things about him. It did not take long for us to realize that we were meant to be together. My advice here is to keep an open mind about what may happen whenever you contact someone or are contacted by someone. It is not possible to know what will happen in every case and pre-judging individuals (within normal limits) may cause you to miss the opportunity of a lifetime. I am not saying ignore your better judgment when certain feelings or circumstances present themselves. I am simply saying, keep an open mind, and do not shut a person whose profile seems interesting down before you actually give yourself an opportunity to explore the possibilities. It is possible that, after the first conversation, you will realize that you have nothing in common with the individual. That is fine; at least you explored the possibilities of a new relationship.

There are reasons why some individuals do not post a photo. Sometimes it is as simple as not having a current photo to post, other times it is that the person does not feel photogenic. It could also be that the person does not want their photo to detract a potential mate's attention with a less than suitable photograph. Or it may be as it seems, the individual is 'hard to look at'. The reality is though that whatever the reason, one cannot know until one tries to get to know the individual better. Besides, beauty is in the eye of the beholder. The

person with no photo
may appear to be gorgeous.

Ask the Tough Questions

Now that we are living in an especially politically correct society, we are often confused about what we can say to a person or if we are even allowed to ask certain questions. Most of us are governed by a strong conscience and a strong awareness or what is polite or impolite. This is something good especially since we want to maintain functional, happy relationships, however, when it comes down to getting to know someone from a distance, some of those built in scruples must be ignored in order to obtain information that would determine if one should continue to pursue a relationship. I would say in this case, if there is something, you would like to know, ask the question. Also, remember to trust but verify. Ask if they have a criminal background; ask how they feel about certain criminal behavior. Ask if they have ever been involved in any type of domestic abuse. Ask about work history; ask about sexual history; ask if they are healthy. Ask if they would be willing to submit to medical tests to confirm their health status. Ask if they have ever been unfaithful to a partner. If there is anything that is important to you, be sure to ask the tough questions. Do not accept non-answers as answers; do not assume you understand the answer. Beware of anyone who goes on the offensive when they are being asked these questions. If the person is truly interested in making a life with you, then he or she would not have a problem answering the questions. If it would help to satisfy your doubts, have a professional background check done to confirm that there is nothing criminal to worry about. As a matter of common sense, one should understand that even if someone does not have a criminal history it does not mean that they have never committed a crime. It could mean that they have never been caught or that they may have sealed records. One should use a clean criminal history in conjunction with observed behavior to determine if an individual is safe.

Do not be afraid to ask about finances. Most of us are independent and can take care of ourselves, but that does not mean we want to be immediately saddled with someone who is looking for a sugar mommy or daddy. One may shy away from asking questions about money because one does not want to seem like a gold-digger, but one needs to know exactly what to expect financially when choosing a mate. I cannot say one should or should not date someone with money; it all depends on what one wants to do in his or her relationship. What I would advise though is for one to make an informed decision when it comes to money. Wealth does not guarantee happiness neither does poverty. For myself, I believe that when one is looking for a spouse one should be able to take care of one's family if need be, but the partner should also be able and willing to do the same. If that is a problem, one should reconsider if they want to be with this person. Love is wonderful, but it does not put food on the table. Relationships are difficult; they do not need the added frustrations that come with money problems. Even if one may be willing to deal with limited financial resources, one may not be prepared to handle the social repercussions of limited finances. One may not be able to go out with friends as one would like or keep up with the 'Joneses' as one may prefer. Today many married couples function as roommates. A roommate relationship is one where both parties split all expenses down the middle while sharing the same bed. Some may even continue their separate lives with the exception of sleeping with their spouse. The roommate relationship often faces major challenges if the employment status of one of the people in the relationship were to change. The other party can become resentful because he or she is now feeling financially burdened by the marriage responsibility. One party may feel that the other owes them and that they are feeling unappreciated and taken advantage of. Couples need to discuss and decide ahead of time of this is the type of relationship they want to have. Although being roommates can be fun and efficient, the interactions of roommates may not be practical for married people and in the long-term may do more harm than good to the relationship. As taxing as financial issues may be, they are not the only reason why relationships fail.

Religion is another topic people shy away from, but if religion is important to you, ask about it. Whether that means you want someone with your same beliefs or you want someone with no beliefs. It is important and should be discussed at length especially if you plan to have future children together. Marriagepreparation.com (1996), cites a few paragraphs which say

["One recent study indicates a 75% failure rate for interfaith marriages – 50% higher than for American marriages overall. This may be due to the fact that, as we have observed, many young couples marry without really understanding what their own unexamined assumptions can do to the fabric of a marriage. Adding the tensions of different faiths to all the other pulls increases the odds of ending up

with tatters [in pieces] – unless you learn to pull together.

[Many people writing about interfaith marriage, avoid talking about God because they think that will only add to the differences, but] "… We think this is a mistake. While a certain surface stability may be achieved by one or both partners' ignoring the part God plays in their lives, they're missing a chance to weave a strong, beautifully patterned web. As it says in the Book of Ecclesiastes: 'Two are better than one….and a threefold cord will not be broken.' Recognizing the sacred character of marriage will give your relationship strength for the long haul." (Celebrating our Differences: Living Two Faiths in

One Marriage, Stanley & Mary Rosenbaum 1999, p. 1.)] It does not make sense to avoid the topic when seeking a spouse because religious differences will likely end your marriage. Religion in itself is important in any relationship, but religion often shapes the way people think relationships ought to be. Religion dictates how people live their lives and would have a significant impact on any relationship. One would not like to end up in a relationship with someone who has opposite religious beliefs. It would result in major personal battles of conscience and culminate in fights, arguments, and finally a broken relationship. Although it is possible for a person to change, when it comes to religious beliefs, the changes to be made would need to be major especially if the belief spectrum is far apart. A Christian person would probably not make it with an atheist or a Muslim or Hindu etc. Speak in-depth about religion and religious beliefs. Many say they are not religious, but that they are spiritual; find out what that means and what it entails. Do not make any assumptions about what a person means when it comes to such an important topic.

During my quest to find the love of my life, I was contacted by a man who said he was a minister. We had a discussion about crime, prison, and the people who are incarcerated. He shared with me that although he had never been to prison, he believed that 99% of the people in prison were innocent. Now, that comment suggested a few things to me about that man:

1. He is crazy,
2. He has been to prison or
3. He is trying to make himself look innocent for something he did, but is not ready to admit.

Needless to say that was my final conversation with that person. I just could not wrap my mind around his comment, and I decided then that I was not willing to explore the possibilities with him.

Someone else may have made a different choice than I did in that situation, but I was not prepared to waste my time on a relationship that was not going to go anywhere and was clearly based on some sinister, hidden information. My advice would be not to be paranoid, but if it doesn't seem right, then it probably isn't. We were all given instincts for our protection, do not ignore them.

He or she has children. What now?

Dating someone with children presents a whole different world of circumstances. It is something that should be seriously considered before one invests too much emotionally in a relationship. Of course circumstances vary depending on the age of the child or children involved, and the challenges vary depending on the age of the children, but there will still be challenges even if one has his or her own children.

As with any relationship, a child may 'cramp' the style

of new lovers. A child needs attention and parents generally put their children first. What this may mean for your relationship is that even if you want alone time with your lover, he or she may not be as free to spend that time with you because there is a child to take care of. There is also the added challenge of getting the child or children to accept a new person in their life/lives. Not every child is willing to see another person fill the role of their mother or father. This does not mean one should write off relationships with people who have children, it just warrants serious consideration. Most people are aware of their limits when it comes to an issue as serious as children, so if one is honest enough with oneself this should not be a tough decision to make. There is an old saying that you should keep in mind, it says that 'you cannot want the cow if you do not want the calf.'

In an article, Kamau (2008) wrote the following, [Relationships are complex on their own, but adding children to the mix can make things a good deal more complicated.

A lot of people avoid potential dates with children and single parents are often quite nervous about dating. The emotions of everyone involved, including the children, must be considered.

Do not rush to meet your date's children, but do not avoid it either. Generally, you should focus on developing a relationship with your love interest first before taking the step of becoming involved, even briefly, with the children. If the relationship only lasts a brief time, it can be confusing and upsetting for the children when you are close with their parent and then suddenly are no longer around.

Once you have met the children and become involved in their life, it is essential to consider the situation and the children's feelings. It is a good idea to discuss what your partner may expect of you in relation to their children. Some people may be looking for you to be a parental figure, while others may explicitly discourage you from trying to take such a role.

Remember that while you are now dating their mother or father, they still have another parent, and it is important that expectations are clear between you and their parent. If you both do not have a clear expectation, it may be very bewildering for the children.

It is vital to build a good relationship with the children as you move into a commitment with their mother or father. Be careful as some children may resent your presence, feeling as though you are trying to replace their other parent. This can cause children to lash out in mean, hurtful and angry ways.

You and your partner need to be understanding and help the children adjust to your relationship. It can be very helpful to have a "family pow-wow", sitting down with your lover and their children to discuss roles, boundaries and expectations. This helps the children feel engaged, giving them a sense of control and input into the situation.

After you have developed a good relationship with the children, it is important to keep working on the relationship between you and their parent. With time, the difficulties will fade, and you together act more and more like a "true" family. Dating a single parent can be difficult at times, but very rewarding. Keep this advice on dating someone with children in mind and it will help ease any difficulties, leading to a happy relationship and happy family.]

Incidentally, I married a man who already had a son, but our circumstances are in my opinion not ordinary because my step-son is almost grown up. That means I do not have a great deal of parenting to do. I will not claim to be a person who knows the best thing to do in a situation where you inherit children, but consider what you can learn about your potential partner or spouse from the behavior of the child or children. If one is looking for signs regarding the type of parent a partner might be or about their parenting skills, discoveries made while observing the children and the interaction with their parents are invaluable.

Blending families is difficult. The love between two people would need to be strong to aid in a successful combination of families. Children can make a relationship difficult even when both parents (stepparents) are in agreement as to how to parent the children. Then there is the added friction from the birth parent that does not live in the primary residence. When one is seeking a mate online, one should be sure to establish the parameters of the relationship in regard to existing children so that one can decide if one is willing to deal with a ready-made family. If one has reservations about children and cannot resolve them, one should stay away from a potential mate with kids because it only increases the difficulty in the relationship. When one is dating with kids, the children often 'interrupts' the dating process as well, so for someone who needs the undivided attention of a potential partner, this is not the way to go. That being said; one should not just write-off someone with children before considering the pros and cons. If the person in whom you are interested is perfect for you except for being a parent, one should weigh the odds before discarding a possible soul mate.

What to do when your 'love' is far away?

One of the toughest challenges in an internet or long-distance relationship and any relationship for that matter is keeping the communication flowing. Daily communication will keep the relationship current and growing. Use whatever medium is at your disposal in order to keep the lines of communication open. Keep in touch as often as you would have if the person were next door or maybe even more than that. Keeping in touch lets your special someone know that you are interested and yearning for communication with them. Please note that even though you should use every mode of communication that is at your disposal, not every mode of communication is appropriate for every circumstance. Do not use texting as a means of avoiding one on one communication. Texting is great for short messages but should not be looked at as any real form of communication. You cannot get to know a person better through texting, and you cannot bond spiritually through texting. Skyping or telephoning can build a personal bond as you would be able to see the individual and hear his or her voice. According to Githinji, [This will make them feel a part of it, and they will have no reason to doubt you. Avoid calling for a millisecond thinking that you are saving money. In the end, you could be ending your relationship. Designate time in which you will call your partner and talk for hours. You can not see them, but you can hear them. Be a keen listener that way, you can almost tell whether your partner is okay or is having trouble wherever he or she is. That way, you will grow even closer and your long distance relationship will work.] Do not become a stalker. Remember this person, wherever he or she is has responsibilities and routines which must continue regardless of your relationship. Take those things into consideration when deciding what the frequency and length of your communications should be. Make sure that both parties agree to all modes of communication and the frequency. Use your knowledge of the individual to determine if this is reasonable. Always be respectful. Do not call at "booty call" hours unless given the okay to do so.

Please show real interest in the person's life while sharing things about yourself. Share your daily experiences with each other. Remember the person is not with you physically so he or she cannot experience your days, you must verbalize your experiences so that your special someone would become a part of your everyday experiences. Longdistancerelationships.com states, [A common worry among couples in long distance relationships, is that their partner (or that they themselves) will have an affair while they're separated. Common sense suggests that because partners can't keep an eye on one another they might be more prone to wander. Researchers have examined whether couples in long distance relationships have more affairs than geographically close couples. These studies produced both good news and bad. The good news is that all three studies showed that couples in long distance relationships had no greater risk of having an affair than geographically close couples. It seems that the risk of having an affair is related more to the quality of the relationship between the couple, and the personalities involved than on mere opportunity.

Now for the bad news: despite what the statistics say, those in long distance relationships worry much more about affairs than those in geographically close relationships.] Knowing this information should help you to worry less, however, please pay attention to your relationship; do not ignore warning signs that something may be wrong. Just be confident in the notion that even if that person were in your same geographical area, had he or she been given the same opportunity, the results would have been the same.

How Would I know if He/She Really Loves me?

Recognizing love is a very important part of making a relationship work. Once one realizes that love is happening, or has happened, then comes the decision making part. So what does one do when one chooses to love another? What one does here, or thinks of doing at this point, is a test as to whether or not what one is feeling is really love. Many poets and song writers have written verses and stanzas regarding the unparalleled greatness of love, but the truth is that love forces us to make tough choices and decisions. John Seabrook in a poem called "Missing You" wrote,

[*My heart aches within from missing you,
My lips long for the feel of kissing you,*

*Right now all I need is to gently touch your skin,
To look into your eyes and see deep within,
Just one warm embrace,
Just to look upon your face,
Just one little touch,
From the one I love so much,
If I could gaze upon your smile,
For just a little while,
To know that you miss me too,
As I'm thinking of you,
To hear the sound of you breathe,
Knowing you'll never leave,*

To see you walk up to me,
Then embrace you tenderly,
To just be with the one who's sent my heart reeling,
And brought about this downpour of emotion and feeling,
I sit here alone in my office tonight,
And pray that somehow this all turns out right,
I've never been one to do more taking than giving,
I'm not well off but I work hard for a living,
I've told you many thoughts that weren't borrowed or bought,
And in lifetime, who would have thought,
That I have found someone who was just meant for me,
I can't explain the magic or why

this should be, But there is one thing that I know for certain, That this just isn't over till one of us draws the final curtain, For I've seen an angel and I want you to know, If it's my choice to make, I'll never let you go, Don't know what life holds, maybe there's no reason or rhyme, To think you may be mine in a matter of time, And though I cannot touch you and we are now apart, My Love, you do dwell, so deep within my heart.]

As romantic as the poem is, love has a great deal to do with giving of oneself and compromising. When one loves, one does not feel comfortable with not making plans for the future with that special person. This is especially true when there is a vast distance between "lovers". Future plans do not include phone calls, text messages, or dinner dates. Future plans include long-distance planned visits, long-term plans to eliminate the long-distance status. Nothing says you are serious about a relationship more than your willingness to remove the long-distance status from a relationship. If one is as committed as one believes, it will not be a difficult step to take for either party. It will simply be a matter of when.

This type of planning will also move the relationship into the next stage, the stage of joining families. This is where engagement happens, and marriage plans are made. Love encompasses a great deal of emotions, but it is quite amazing because true love grows as one gets to know more about a potential mate. A person's definition of love can make a humongous difference in whether or not a relationship works. I have heard the comment time and again about people growing apart or not finding each other attractive any more. When you love someone you don't grow apart, growing apart is a choice. Whenever one partner chooses to go in one direction and is not concerned about whether the other partner wants to go in that direction, then it is safe to say love is not what that partner is feeling. This does not mean that there are no amicable feelings for one's partner; it just means that there is not enough "love" for that other partner to be less selfish about his or her desires.

Some partners say they are no longer attracted to their mate. Sometimes this is due to one partner gaining weight or the partner getting grey hair. Both of those issues that I just mentioned are superficial, and if they are important enough, both partners can work on them to change the situation.

How a person feels about the previous step would have a large impact on how he or she goes about locking down his or her relationship. It is at this stage that fears and doubts prevail. Many at this time may say that they do not know the person enough or that not enough time has passed to make a long-term commitment, but here is where a reality check is needed. Remember, the geographical distance between you does not make your relationship any less successful than relationships without that factor. Consider that people who know and have known each other for years still break-up. So time does not guarantee a more successful relationship. This is not to say one has to be careless about a decision of such magnitude; it is simply a means of putting things into perspective. This is especially true since many bystanders will be sure to point out that you may be rushing into a situation. Generally, decent men and women are not interested in dating multiple people. They know what they want, and they are simply seeking someone with matching ideals. Once they find that someone, unless there is something obviously wrong, they are usually ready to take a chance on that person and settle down. Whenever one finds the person that he or she considers to be the perfect match, one does not usually want to wait to make plans for the future. If the person chosen shares your level of commitment, then that individual would also prefer not to wait any longer than it is necessary to make wedding plans.

When I met my husband in person for the first time, I was excited and frightened. I was afraid that he would be disappointed in me; I was concerned that, after meeting me in person, he would simply return home and slowly disappear from my life. By the way, if after you meet your love in person and the communication dwindles, something is wrong. The communication should get stronger, not weaker. After I met my husband, he told me it would break his heart if he had to leave me without making permanent plans for the future. That was one of the happiest moments in my life, just knowing that he felt the same way. Needless to say, he asked me to marry him right away, and I said 'yes'. Please note, we spent many hours getting to know each other via various modes of communication and so we knew each other quite well by the time we met each other in person.

You may be saying, "'wow' this author is crazy", but I promise you that it works. It worked for me ,and it worked for my sister as well as countless others. Do not be fooled, love is on the internet; however, one just needs to be able to recognize it so that it can work. Do not be careless with your life; make sure both you and your partner are well before you engage in activities which can spread disease. It is a sign of respect to care about each other that way.

One final word of advice, when you get married, remember marriage takes work. Being in love is just the beginning. Be prepared to expect challenges in your relationship the same way you experience challenges in your other relationships. Most challenges are frivolous and are easy to resolve; it just depends on what one wants. A married friend told me to expect challenges especially early in the relationship. Patience is very important when nurturing a new relationship. This is especially difficult for those of us who are accustomed to living alone and have done so for a long time. When one is “set” in his or her ways change becomes difficult and can produce stress on the relationship. One has to be willing to accept a certain degree of stress as normal while each partner adjusts to living together. This is due to the fact that it will be your first time living together and adjusting into each other’s spaces and comfort zone. One also has to be willing to leave his or her past experiences in the past and focus completely on the relationship at hand. Comparing the current relationship to a past relationship may be detrimental to the new and budding romance. That being said if one notices red flags in the new relationship, one should not ignore them.

Do I have any regrets?

I have been married to my soul mate for the past 4 years. We expanded our family with a new baby. We are looking forward to all the possibilities that we would encounter as life goes on, and we look forward to facing all of our challenges together. We feel truly blessed to have met each other, and we feel blessed to have our son. My only regret is that it took us, so long to find each other. I believe that the time it took us to find each other was the time we needed for God to prepare us for each other.

Many things may be out of our control, but one still has to take action in order to make some things happen. Mr. or Mrs. Right may be around the corner, but he or she may also be a click away. There really is only one way to find out…you have to try.

The views expressed in this book are based on my experiences, the experiences of close friends and some research. Many people have been open in explaining their adventures to me on this subject. The reports vary from that of being blissful and fairytale to tragic and terrifying. I wrote this book with the expectation that people would have a better chance to avoid the dangers and heartbreaks that are inherent to meeting strangers. My hope is that people can someday feel more comfortable and secure about online dating because online dating presents opportunities that one would not readily find elsewhere. I believe this could open many more opportunities for the possibility of finding true love. A person no longer has to settle for the only available boy or girl in town. The internet offers options.

Good luck to you. I hope this book helps you find and keep true love.

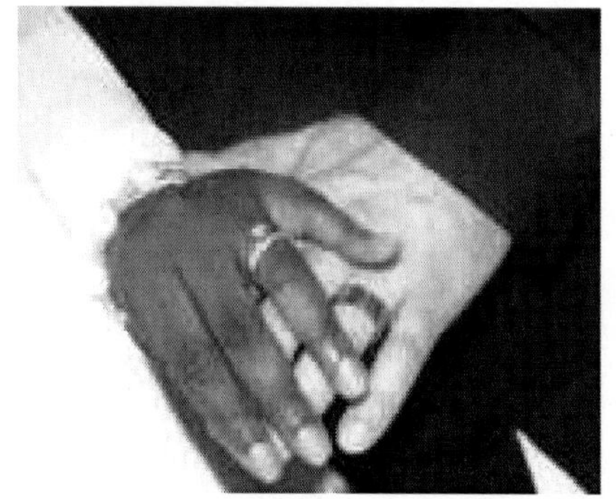

Bibliography

DuPraw, M.E & Axner, M. (1997). Working on Common Cross-Cultural Communication Challenges. http://www.pbs.org/ampu/crosscult.html#FTNT5

Githinji, F.K. (2010). Make long distance relationships work. http://www.ideamarketers.com/? Make Long Distance Relationship Work &articleid=405952

Kamau, D. N. (2008). Dating a Single Parent - Advice For Dating Someone With

Children. http://ezinearticles.com/?Dating-a-Single-Parent---Advice-For-Dating-Someone-With-Children&id=1256394

Langemeier, L. (2011). Lending Rules: Money, Family and Friends. http://liveoutloud.com/drphil/articles/lending-money-rules.php

Lantieri, L. & Patti, J. (1996). Waging Peace in Our Schools. Beacon Press. http://www.pbs.org/ampu/crosscult.html#FTNT_5

Long distance relationships, do they

work? (2010). www.longdistancerelationships.com

Mixed Religion Marriage: Interfaith/Interchurch Marriage. (1996). http://www.marriagepreparation.com/Mixed_religion_marriage.htm

Pagels, D. (1950). To the one person I consider to be My Soul Mate: Love messages meant to be shared with a very special person. Blue Mountain Press. SPS. Studios. Colorado.

Seabrook, J. (1999). Missing You. http://100-

poems.com/poems/love/1338001.htm...John

Sullivan, Bob.(2005). Seduced into scams: Online lovers often duped.Dating sites, singles chat rooms latest target of Nigerian scams. Http://www.msnbc.msn.com/id/8704213/